my big

# brother

by Valorie Fisher

AN ANNE SCHWARTZ BOOK

Atheneum Books for Young Readers

New York London Toronto Sydney Singapore

ACKNOWLEDGMENTS

Thanks to Karen Hatt, Matt Mitler, Theresa Urbano, Henry Horenstein, and the most patient of
dogs, Beanie, for their help in creating this book. And special thanks to Anne Schwartz, Lee Wade,
and my husband, David, for their generous enthusiasm.

Atheneum Books for Young Readers
An imprint of Simon & Schuster Children's Publishing Division
1230 Avenue of the Americas
New York, New York 10020
Copyright © 2002 by Valorie Fisher
All rights reserved, including the right
of reproduction in whole or in part in any form.
Book design by Lee Wade
The text of this book is set in Aunt Mildred.
Printed in Hong Kong
2  4  6  8  10  9  7  5  3  1
Library of Congress Cataloging-in-Publication Data
Fisher, Valorie.
My big brother / by Valorie Fisher.
p. cm.  "An Anne Schwartz book."
Summary: Photographs and simple text depict
a big brother from the point of
view of his baby sibling.
ISBN 0-689-84327-5
[1. Brothers—Fiction.] I. Title.
PZ7.F53485 My 2002
[E]—dc21    2001022947

FIRST
EDITION

For Aidan and Olive

This is my
big brother.

Everyone makes a
fuss over how big I am,
but my brother is
REALLY big.

He can do the most amazing things.

He has a very
important job,

and some very
funny friends.

Still, he always finds time to play with me.

My big brother
feeds me,

and I feed my
big brother.

My big brother

makes the best music.

I like to sing along.

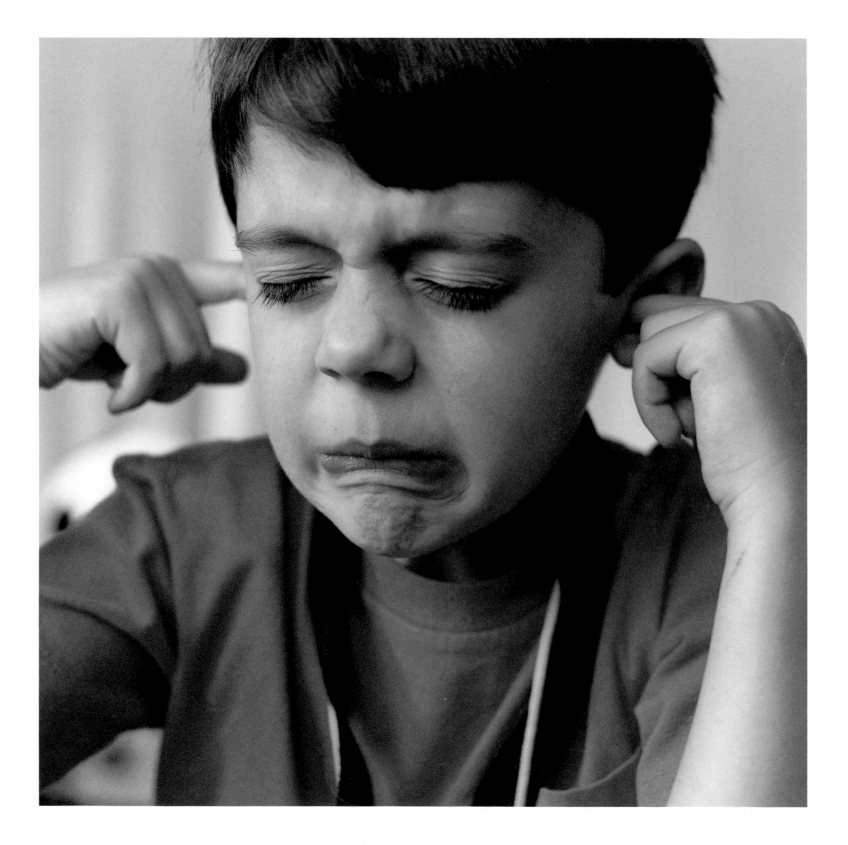

He tells me

he is training

for the circus.

Sometimes I can't
find him anywhere,

and then like

magic he appears.

I love my
big brother,

and he loves me.